About the Author

The author, aside from his name, wishes to remain in anonymity. Instead, allow the stories that unfold in the pages of his work to tell the tale of who he is and where he is going. With the right set of eyes, you'll know him well enough. You'll hear him in the echoes of hard times. You'll feel him next to you when you have a hangover. You'll see him looking back at you in the mirror when you've lost everything. Remember, the brighter the fires of fiction, the smaller the shadows are for truth to hide in.

# The West Mulberry Street Diaries

D. William L.

The West Mulberry Street Diaries

Olympia Publishers
London

www.olympiapublishers.com
OLYMPIA PAPERBACK EDITION

Copyright © D. William L. 2024

The right of D. William L. to be identified as author of
this work has been asserted in accordance with sections 77 and 78
of the Copyright, Designs and Patents Act 1988.

All Rights Reserved

No reproduction, copy or transmission of this publication
may be made without written permission.
No paragraph of this publication may be reproduced,
copied or transmitted save with the written permission of the
publisher, or in accordance with the provisions
of the Copyright Act 1956 (as amended).

Any person who commits any unauthorised act in relation to
this publication may be liable to criminal
prosecution and civil claims for damage.

A CIP catalogue record for this title is
available from the British Library.

ISBN: 978-1-80074-553-7

This is a work of fiction.
Names, characters, places and incidents originate from the writer's
imagination. Any resemblance to actual persons, living or dead, is
purely coincidental.

First Published in 2024

Olympia Publishers
Tallis House
2 Tallis Street
London
EC4Y 0AB

Printed in Great Britain

PREFACE

This preface (sort of) was felt to be mildly necessary due to the following story's uncommon (and slightly punchy) mode and method. Before I crash-landed on W. Mulberry Street (city undisclosed), I was a painter. I spoke through color. Following a series of what should be considered inevitable life hurdles and failing to jump high enough when I approached them, I lost my home, my painting studio and everything else that wouldn't fit into a small box and duffle bag. My few precious books were among those meager properties. Had someone told me of the coming trials that were about to befall me, I'd have likely overcome, and still been a painter. (I understand this is all very vague, but this is not an autobiography.) In the deep end of this pool of involuntary bohemianism, sleeping on an army cot in someone else's one room efficiency (to whom I owe my survival), and diving head first to the bottom of every bottle within reach, my greatest friends, my eternal mistresses to follow, would be my books. It was through the eyes of Charles Bukowski, Victor Hugo, Richard Adams, Italo Svevo and so many others, that I was awoken to this new vocation, and to the recognition of the things that really matter. Those pieces of ourselves that can never be taken away.

The following tales are my attempts to create a cinematograph of sorts, of the distinctive gradations of both my state of mind, and the characters I encountered while living on W. Mulberry Street as best I could, through the eyes of this part factual, part conceived character that I felt my situation was embodying. A consequential voice that was maturing beneath the surface of my circumstances.

The *West Mulberry Street Diaries* are the first of a series of stories that allow the reader to follow the lives of several drunken ne'er-do-wells through the eyes of their very sober journals. It should be noted that the events that transpire may or may not be true. In addition, with regards to the factual events, certain elements have been carefully worded, and in a few cases, slightly embellished. But only to the extent of attempting to convey a specific state of mind or emotion that the protagonist felt when an event took place. Also, names have been changed.

The *West Mulberry Street Diaries* part one and two are the recorded accounts of Wolfgang, a drunken, impoverished, sex-starved poet as he drags himself through his blurry days in section eight housing, rousing only to dissect a feeling or event, or to have a drink.

A separate related short, titled *Madd Man*, has been included as a supplemental story, which is one of the short works that Wolfgang was working on in various entries throughout *The Diaries*. The author (that's me) thought the reader might enjoy reading some of Wolfgang's actual prosaic work, though the reader does get to see some of his poetry throughout the journal.

D. William L.

WEDNESDAY
01.04 a.m. — Hit and run on the corner. Poor bastards. New bottle.

THURSDAY
08.20 p.m. — Wrote out a poem on the burdens of being lonely. How original of me. Wrote out another poem immediately after on growing old. I am on some sort of roll here.

FRIDAY
02.07 a.m. — Finally completed *Love in the Time of Cholera*. This makes five books this month. I never have sex.

SUNDAY
07.00 p.m. — Slept through most of Christmas Eve, so I am feeling rather accomplished.

09.50 p.m. — Visited Von Godi at his sister's home for the purpose of fulfilling my daily alcohol requirements. Von Godi promised me that I would not be accosted by the presence of any family holiday rituals but failed to keep said promise. Fortunately, I was only subjected to the event's closing activities and a few awkward hugs. Von Godi and I fled the scene a few hours later with the aid of vodka and cocaine.

MONDAY
03.20 a.m. — Christmas Day. Made coffee. Had a few cigarettes. Picked up where I left off on Herbert

Marcuse's *Eros and Civilization*. Completed two chapters before I swapped the coffee for wine. New bottle.

11.02 p.m. — Woke up again, despite my best efforts. Started outlining the first twenty-eight chapters of a book I am successfully putting off.

11.50 p.m. — Soaked myself in a nice hot bubble bath with a joint and some Tom Waits. I must ensure I don't overexert myself, you know.

03.30 a.m. — Published two more poems for public ridicule. I am going back to bed.

THURSDAY
08.00 p.m. — Byron and I attended a going away party for a mutual friend, Arthur, who is moving out of state to help someone start a bar in some picturesque mountain town somewhere. We didn't stay too long. Toward the end of the night, Samantha, also a mutual friend and local civil rights activist, gave a drunken, long-winded goodbye speech that seemed to detail every known moment of her and Arthur's friendship. Byron and I took that as our cue to find a new establishment. After a few more bars, we ended up at Thomas' house, who is a rather famous local artist. A small roster of cocktails and a handful of painkillers aided me in noticing that I was presently in the company of every woman in town that I had a crush on. I had to get the fuck out of there.

FRIDAY
02.41 a.m. — Another hit and run. This time they hit my neighbor's Lincoln that was parked on the street, got out, and just ran the fuck away. Police found two of the three assholes that fled.

02.58 a.m. — New bottle.

SUNDAY
01.15 a.m. — There is this drunk college girl passed out in the little courtyard next to my building. I tried shooing it away, but it is unconscious. I have started tossing little pieces of salmon around her from my second story balcony to see what sort of wildlife I can attract.

05.20 p.m. — Woke up. Again. Cigarettes and wine make an okay breakfast.

06.11 p.m. — Started reading *The Greek Alexander Romance*.

10.20 p.m. — Finished reading *The Greek Alexander Romance*. What a shit story. I am out of wine. Going back to bed.

MONDAY
02.40 p.m.— Von Godi came by to borrow a VHS film. I was moving one of my paintings to the kitchen that had finally dried after over a year. (Cheap watercolor will stay wet for ages on the right type of canvas.) I used this same method on a beautiful heart painting that I had in a gallery

downtown, mostly in the hopes that the buyer would assume the work was dry, and then carelessly mess it up by treating it roughly, just like people do with real hearts. It really was a beautiful painting.

"You're an artist. You should do a painting of a dick or something. Be edgy," Von Godi advised.

"I don't know, man. I think it may be a little too early in my career for that sort of thing. I like writing more anyway. It's a lot harder to make your own interpretations with someone's actual words. That's the point of language, both written and spoken, isn't it? To be understood? That's why religions and their bibles are so fucked up. People seem to be free to make their own interpretations. I say, interpret one of my paintings all you want, but don't fuck with my words."

08.00 p.m. — Walking to the corner store for more wine and coffee. It would be nice to have a small apartment above a corner store, or a nice, quiet dive bar.

08.49 p.m. — Wrote out two more poems. Not publishing either one.

09.01 p.m. — My fat cat, Moscow, won't quit meowing. I am going to drink on my bed until I fall asleep.

THURSDAY
02.40 p.m. — Woke up with a rather impressive hangover. I am actually a little concerned that this doesn't happen more often. Oh well. New bottle.

04.01 p.m. — Wrote out another poem about loneliness.

05.21 p.m. — I am sitting naked at my typewriter, eating orange flavored chocolates and drinking wine. Ha!

FRIDAY
07.00 p.m. — Dinner party at Byron's home. Everyone brought something. I brought five bottles of wine. (It's my signature dish.) I only really knew three out of the thirty people there. Byron, of course, his lovely girlfriend and journalist, Christina, and one of our local bartenders, Mackenzie. It was an interesting dinner party. There was French music, Filipino food, a Mayan witch doctor who liked to breastfeed her six year old openly, a very polite and friendly drag queen, a few artists, a little grass, a lot of booze and a cat the size of my drinking problem named Montezuma. It was an interesting dinner party.

SATURDAY
09.10 a.m. — Why in the unholy fuck am I awake this early? I am going to drink myself back to sleep. I hope this never happens again.

SUNDAY
05.40 p.m. — Began reading *The Dunciad Variorum*, written in 1729. That's one thousand seven hundred twenty-nine for all you common folk.

08.52 p.m. — Heading to the bar.

MONDAY
04.30 p.m. — I should probably take a shower at some point.

09.58 p.m. — I have been listening to the same Mendelssohn record for nine days now. I just keep flipping the record over and over. I think it complements the repetitive gray skies of early January so romantically.

11.14 p.m. — Sweet red, cigarettes and the third partition of *The Anatomy of Melancholy* by Robert Burton for lunch. I cannot declare with any certainty that I will ever have sex again. At least I will be drunk.

TUESDAY
12.11 a.m. — If I leave now, I can make it to the bar and still have two good hours of drinking time before they close.

04.50 p.m. — Still haven't taken a shower, but I am pretty drunk. So that's something.

06.01 p.m. — Third bottle of wine today. I have multiple talents.

WEDNESDAY
01.20 a.m. — Fell back asleep. Still haven't taken a shower. I still haven't had sex.

04.30 p.m. — Time to take a red nap.

THURSDAY
05.50 p.m. — Another gray morning. Another red breakfast.

05.59 p.m. — I turned thirty-seven today. Maybe I'll take a shower to commemorate the occasion. I think I'll have a drink first. New poem.

I do not bewail that transient era that was my youth. For in it, I was blind to the grandeur that is life. I was ignorant to its importance. Beholden to no real strength, wisdom or virtue, I possessed no constitution that would urge or encourage me to continue to love, even in the darkest depths of love's absence. My frivolous existence bore no understanding of the gravity of human life, the influence of trust or the sageness of compassion. Tomorrow was assumed to be guaranteed and there was no urgency to my short time alive. All that was before my eyes, the very air in my lungs, those who stood beside me and those now gone, were all taken for granted. Tonight, these cold bitter winds blow the amber coals of my evening cigarette back upon my face as unwelcomely as the unwanted memories of my imbecilic youth. I miss it not. Let the clock spin. Bring me those ephemeral decades, for they only make the wine taste sweeter.

FRIDAY
07.40 p.m. — Started re-reading the collected writings of Ulrike Meinhof. A small but intelligent collection of Marxist fueled essays, written by Meinhof when she was still a journalist.

11.40 p.m. — There is a small flock of lesbians who live in the corner house across the street. They are always getting drunk and fighting each other. I can hear them from my desk just now. This fight is a big one. Slapping sounds, sounds of bodies being slammed into walls and onto pavement, lots of fuck words, patio furniture being smashed and bottles being broken. They seem very energetic. I wonder if they like Beethoven.

SATURDAY
04.02 p.m. — I have two cats, Moscow and Amos. The latter is kind of retarded. Chases imaginary bugs, runs face first into walls, things of that nature. The other, I just learned, has some rare form of cat cancer. Tumors all over his body. Moscow is the most intelligent and emotionally intuitive cat I have ever known. He is also the fattest, weighing in at almost twenty pounds. He walks with the strut of a lion. Far too sweet to deserve cancer. This is going to cost a fortune.

SUNDAY
I just did a bunch of cocaine. I just did a bunch of cocaine.

I just did a bunch of cocaine. I just did a bunch of cocaine.
I just did a bunch of cocaine. I just did a bunch of cocaine.
I just did a bunch of cocaine. I just did a bunch of cocaine.
I just did a bunch of cocaine. I just did a bunch of cocaine.
I just did a bunch of cocaine. I just did a bunch of cocaine.
I just did a bunch of cocaine. I just did a bunch of cocaine.
I just did a bunch of cocaine. I just did a bunch of cocaine.
I just did a bunch of cocaine. I just did a bunch of cocaine.
I just did a bunch of cocaine. I just did a bunch of cocaine.
I just did a bunch of cocaine. I just did a bunch of cocaine.
I just did a bunch of cocaine. I just did a bunch of cocaine.
I just did a bunch of cocaine. I just did a bunch of cocaine.
I just did a bunch of cocaine. I just did a bunch of cocaine.
I just did a bunch of cocaine. I just did a bunch of cocaine.
I just did a bunch of cocaine. I just did a bunch of cocaine.
I just did a bunch of cocaine. I just did a bunch of cocaine.
I just did a bunch of cocaine. I just did a bunch of cocaine.
I just did a bunch of cocaine. I just did a bunch of cocaine.
I just did a bunch of cocaine. I just did a bunch of cocaine.
I just did a bunch of cocaine. I just did a bunch of cocaine.
I just did a bunch of cocaine. I just did a bunch of cocaine.
I just did a bunch of cocaine. I just did a bunch of cocaine.
I just did a bunch of cocaine. I just did a bunch of cocaine.
I just did a bunch of cocaine. I just did a bunch of cocaine.
I just did a bunch of cocaine. I just did a bunch of cocaine.
I just did a bunch of cocaine. I just did a bunch of cocaine.
I just did a bunch of cocaine. I just did a bunch of cocaine.
I just did a bunch of cocaine. I just did a bunch of cocaine.
I just did a bunch of cocaine. I just did a bunch of cocaine.
I just did a bunch of cocaine. I just did a bunch of cocaine.
I just did a bunch of cocaine. I just did a bunch of cocaine.
I just did a bunch of cocaine. I just did a bunch of cocaine.

I just did a bunch of cocaine. I just did a bunch of cocaine.
I just did a bunch of cocaine. I just did a bunch of cocaine.
I just did a bunch of cocaine. I just did a bunch of cocaine.
I just did a bunch of cocaine. I just did a bunch of cocaine.
I just did a bunch of cocaine. I just did a bunch of cocaine.
I just did a bunch of cocaine. I just did a bunch of cocaine.
I just did a bunch of cocaine. I just did a bunch of cocaine.
I just did a bunch of cocaine. I just did a bunch of cocaine.
I just did a bunch of cocaine. I just did a bunch of cocaine.
I just did a bunch of cocaine. I just did a bunch of cocaine.
I just did a bunch of cocaine. I just did a bunch of cocaine.
I just did a bunch of cocaine. I just did a bunch of cocaine.
I just did a bunch of cocaine. I just did a bunch of cocaine.
I just did a bunch of cocaine. I just did a bunch of cocaine.
I just did a bunch of cocaine. I just did a bunch of cocaine.
I just did a bunch of cocaine. I just did a bunch of cocaine.
I just did a bunch of cocaine. I just did a bunch of cocaine.
I just did a bunch of cocaine. I just did a bunch of cocaine.
I just did a bunch of cocaine. I just did a bunch of cocaine.
I just did a bunch of cocaine. I just did a bunch of cocaine.
I just did a bunch of cocaine. I just did a bunch of cocaine.
I just did a bunch of cocaine. I just did a bunch of cocaine.
I just did a bunch of cocaine. I just did a bunch of cocaine.
I just did a bunch of cocaine. I just did a bunch of cocaine.
I just did a bunch of cocaine. I just did a bunch of cocaine.
I just did a bunch of cocaine. I just did a bunch of cocaine.
I just did a bunch of cocaine. I just did a bunch of cocaine.
I just did a bunch of cocaine. I just did a bunch of cocaine.
I just did a bunch of cocaine. I just did a bunch of cocaine.
I just did a bunch of cocaine. I just did a bunch of cocaine.

I just did a bunch of cocaine. I just did a bunch of cocaine.
I just did a bunch of cocaine. I just did a bunch of cocaine.
I just did a bunch of cocaine. I just did a bunch of cocaine.
I just did a bunch of cocaine. I just did a bunch of cocaine.
I just did a bunch of cocaine. I just did a bunch of cocaine.
I just did a bunch of cocaine. I just did a bunch of cocaine.
I just did a bunch of cocaine. I just did a bunch of cocaine.
I just did a bunch of cocaine. I just did a bunch of cocaine.
I just did a bunch of cocaine. I just did a bunch of cocaine.
I just did a bunch of cocaine. I just did a bunch of cocaine.
I just did a bunch of cocaine. I just did a bunch of cocaine.
I just did a bunch of cocaine. I just did a bunch of cocaine.
I just did a bunch of cocaine. I just did a bunch of cocaine.
I just did a bunch of cocaine. I just did a bunch of cocaine.
I just did a bunch of cocaine. I just did a bunch of cocaine.
I just did a bunch of cocaine. I just did a bunch of cocaine.
I just did a bunch of cocaine. I just did a bunch of cocaine.
I just did a bunch of cocaine. I just did a bunch of cocaine.
I just did a bunch of cocaine. I just did a bunch of cocaine.
I just did a bunch of cocaine. I just did a bunch of cocaine.
I just did a bunch of cocaine. I just did a bunch of cocaine.
I just did a bunch of cocaine. I just did a bunch of cocaine.
I just did a bunch of cocaine. I just did a bunch of cocaine.
I just did a bunch of cocaine. I just did a bunch of cocaine.
I just did a bunch of cocaine. I just did a bunch of cocaine.
I just did a bunch of cocaine. I just did a bunch of cocaine.
I just did a bunch of cocaine. I just did a bunch of cocaine.
I just did a bunch of cocaine. I just did a bunch of cocaine.
I just did a bunch of cocaine. I just did a bunch of cocaine.
I just did a bunch of cocaine. I just did a bunch of cocaine.

I just did a bunch of cocaine. I just did a bunch of cocaine.
I just did a bunch of cocaine. I just did a bunch of cocaine.
I just did a bunch of cocaine. I just did a bunch of cocaine.
I just did a bunch of cocaine. I just did a bunch of cocaine.
I just did a bunch of cocaine. I just did a bunch of cocaine.
I just did a bunch of cocaine. I just did a bunch of cocaine.
I just did a bunch of cocaine. I just did a bunch of cocaine.
I just did a bunch of cocaine. I just did a bunch of cocaine.
I just did a bunch of cocaine. I just did a bunch of cocaine.
I just did a bunch of cocaine. I just did a bunch of cocaine.
I just did a bunch of cocaine. I just did a bunch of cocaine.
I just did a bunch of cocaine. I just did a bunch of cocaine.
I just did a bunch of cocaine. I just did a bunch of cocaine.
I just did a bunch of cocaine. I just did a bunch of cocaine.
I just did a bunch of cocaine. I just did a bunch of cocaine.
I just did a bunch of cocaine. I just did a bunch of cocaine.
I just did a bunch of cocaine. I just did a bunch of cocaine.
I just did a bunch of cocaine. I just did a bunch of cocaine.
I just did a bunch of cocaine. I just did a bunch of cocaine.
I just did a bunch of cocaine. I just did a bunch of cocaine.
I just did a bunch of cocaine. I just did a bunch of cocaine.
I just did a bunch of cocaine. I just did a bunch of cocaine.
I just did a bunch of cocaine. I just did a bunch of cocaine.
I just did a bunch of cocaine. I just did a bunch of cocaine.
I just did a bunch of cocaine. I just did a bunch of cocaine.
I just did a bunch of cocaine. I just did a bunch of cocaine.
I just did a bunch of cocaine. I just did a bunch of cocaine.
I just did a bunch of cocaine. I just did a bunch of cocaine.
I just did a bunch of cocaine. I just did a bunch of cocaine.
I just did a bunch of cocaine. I just did a bunch of cocaine.
I just did a bunch of cocaine. I just did a bunch of cocaine.

MONDAY
07.12 p.m. — Apparently, it frightens Amos when you subject him to Arnold Schwarzenegger impersonations.

TUESDAY
01.20 a.m. — Had a few drinks at the bar with Juan, Scarlet and 'Chia' Steve, who are bartenders at my most notorious watering hole. Discussed theatre, musicals and the pseudo-bohemian pursuit of cocaine in Austin, Texas during the early days of our college years.

03.38 p.m. — Cigarettes and red for breakfast. Because who here really gives a shit.

05.19 p.m. — Took a shower. It is a pain to do when you don't have hot water. I have to boil the water on my little camping stove and take bucket baths. Shit. I am out of cigarettes.

WEDNESDAY
08.00 a.m. — Despite my firm beliefs that waking up before noon is the sick act of a desperate person, today, I have no choice. Taking Moscow in for surgery to have three large tumors removed. He hates me already.

THURSDAY
06.03 p.m. — Reading *Man of Straw* by Heinrich Mann while my cats stare at me with some sort of contemptuous look on their faces. I have asked them what the problem is, but they are well versed in counter interrogation tactics and are maintaining their silence.

09.20 p.m. — Heading to the bar.

FRIDAY
02.40 a.m. — Home from the bar. New poem. New bottle.

TUESDAY
01.10 p.m. — Taking Moscow to have his stitches removed. Little guy hates riding in cars, and cries whenever the vehicle is in motion.
"MEOW!"
"Yeah, man, I know this sucks. But that's life."
"MEOW."
"Well, this cancer stuff can happen to anyone, really. It will most likely happen to me as well."
"Meow."
"Yep. And then I'll have to go to the doctor too, if I can afford it. Only I won't have anyone to go with me like you do. I'll have to go alone."
"meow."

WEDNESDAY
07.40 p.m. — Stepped out onto my front balcony for a cigarette and found one of my downstairs neighbors (a practitioner of the chemical arts), who we shall call 'Mongoose', sitting on his front stoop in the snow, with his shirt off, eating peanut butter from the jar with a large wooden spoon. Upon seeing me, he very happily exclaimed that he had a present for me. He then ran back inside and re-emerged moments later with a sixties model

Lincoln hubcap and very carefully set it in plain view for me to see. He then ran back inside again, slamming his door and turned off all his lights. About two and a half minutes later, the faint aroma of methamphetamines began to casually emit from his poorly sealed windows. I wonder if I will always retain the fortune that bestows me with friends like Mongoose.

09.20 p.m. — I am out of wine.

10.11 p.m. — I have acquired another bottle of wine.

11.01 p.m. — I am out of wine again.

11.32 p.m. — I now have three bottles of wine. Continuing to read *The Dunciad Variorum*. Early seventeenth century literature isn't always the roller coaster thrill ride you would normally expect.

THURSDAY
02.40 a.m. — Saw an old playwright friend of mine at the bar. He'd written a few good plays around town but moved away to become a paramedic. I guess he needed the money.

01.30 p.m. — New tenants have moved into the house on my corner. Thomas, the artist, used to live there, but moved to the other side of the university in protest of his financial situation. I only caught a glimpse of one of the new inhabitants before he scurried back inside. I hope they aren't dog people.

04.41 p.m. — Wrote out two more poems.

SATURDAY
08.18 a.m. — It would appear I've slept through Friday. Even still, it is too early to be out of bed.

03.27 p.m. — Arose at a more appropriate hour. Refrigerator has died. All that bologna and three-year-old pickle relish may perish if action is not taken. Fortunately, wine does not need to be kept cold. All will not be lost.

04.40 p.m. — I can hear my neighbor masturbating. I really dislike thin walls.

04.58 p.m. — I am out of wine.

05.20 p.m. — Two of my wall outlets have gone out. There are two other outlets — one in the bathroom, and one in the 'living room' that are just exposed circuitry and have been that way since last summer. I really do live the bourgeoisie lifestyle here.

06.11 p.m. — The bars have been open for some time now. I should grace them with my presence.

SUNDAY
03.19 a.m. — There is this barback girl at one of the local holes (we'll call her 'L') who is a wiccan. She wears this big crystal around her neck, and she started explaining

the differences between various crystals. We started talking about geophysics, the earth, and the way sound travels at different speeds through different types of rock. I have a bunch of junk stored in piles all over this shithole of a state. In one of these junk piles, I have a rather large chunk of black tourmaline. I think I will dig that out and give it to L. Perhaps she can use it to cast some sort of spell that will summon one of the bartenders. What I am trying to say here is, my glass is empty.

11.40 p.m. — Went to the bar again. Had an in-depth conversation about astrophysics, the bible and airline tickets. Gave another bartender, who got too drunk, a ride home.

MONDAY
04.21 p.m. — The last two outlets in my cozy little hovel have gone out. Not out of wine yet, however. Focus on the positive.

WEDNESDAY
04.01 a.m. — Still don't have power to my refrigerator. It is presently five degrees outside, so I shouldn't fret. I can store what little food I have on the back porch if needs be. I have heavy patchwork quilts and wine for warmth. I have cigarettes, books and my typewriter for entertainment and candles for light. Not doing too bad here.

05.11 p.m. — Bread is blue. Meat is grey. Onions still look good though. Fuck it. I'm making a sandwich.

06.40 p.m. — New bottle. New poem.

THURSDAY

01.10 p.m. — I was rudely awoken to a chop, chop, chopping sound coming from outside behind my building, accompanied by the ever-literate verbiage of the classic American city worker. I stepped out onto my back balcony, eyebrows raised, manhandling a bottle of wine with a cigarette in my mouth.

"Good morning," I recited sardonically, taking a chest-puffed swig. "What is it exactly that you two are working on?"

"Weer cidy werkers. Weer doon some cidy werk, fer the cidy," he pronounced.

"Ah. I see. Is this for the city then?" I replied, emptying the bottle of its remaining contents down my gullet, then stamping the empty bottle down onto the balcony railing next to a collection of others, and marching back inside to the warm embrace of my low rent nest, I polished off the half drunken bottle of red that was hiding under my pillow, then drifted back to sleep in the comfort of knowing that the infrastructure of this city was being articulately maintained by those two, fine able men. I do hope they are well paid.

05.00 p.m. — Fuck it. I'm just going to start a wine rack.

05.40 p.m. — Arrived at the wine shop in city center.

05.41 p.m. — Laid a large suitcase on the counter, clicked

open its shiny brass button locks and laid bare its large empty belly before the eyes of the unsuspecting clerk.

"Fill 'er up." I charged dutifully.

"Pardon me?"

"I would like this large toting apparatus filled with various wines, please. Reds only."

06.20 p.m. — Arrived home with twenty-eight bottles of wine. Fourteen in the suitcase, one in either coat pocket and the rest in paper bags. What the fuck am I going to do with all these paper bags now?

FRIDAY
04.30 p.m. — I wonder if I should go buy some food?

04.30½ p.m. — New bottle.

09.25 p.m. — Finished reading *Watership Down*. Now that, was truly brilliant writing. I shall de-cork a new bottle to celebrate.

11.12 p.m. — The stars are really out tonight. I found the North Star. What a shitty, dim little fucker it is. Why would you ever choose that for navigation? I mean, I understand why, but visually it's kind of a letdown. New bottle.

11.48 p.m. — Found the Big Dipper. And there is the Little Dipper. And way over there, there is a mid-sized dipper. And over there, there is a saucepan-type dipper. There is a Tupperware dipper next to it.

SATURDAY

01.10 a.m. — Heading to the bar with my neighbor, Ryan.

03.50 a.m. — I just hit and ran a decorative bush in a bar parking lot. I was able to get out of there before any of the other shrubbery got my license plate. Not sure what happened to Ryan. The fucking lilacs may have got him. I am on the lam.

SUNDAY

08.11 p.m. — Last night I drank until I puked. I couldn't even sit at my typewriter.

08.14 p.m. — New bottle. I have holes in my shoes.

MONDAY

04.00 p.m. — Behind my building, there is this decorative (sort of) city drainage ditch, lined with cobblestone. This thing is a major highway for all manner of small, beady-eyed animals. Raccoons, opossums, skunks, rats, interpretive dance students. I should put some traps out.

08.20 p.m. — Von Godi has met a woman. In conjunction with this event, it is my tragic oath to accompany him to the bar (that part isn't so bad) to be his wingman. What the fuck does that even mean? Am I to slump alongside him, 'pretending to be drunk, (my performances are genuine, or not at all.) to make him look better? Do I need to be a yes man of sorts? I have zero experience for this job title. No one ever said, "Hey, there is this really great girl I'd like to get to know. I should bring Wolfgang along to make a good impression." Do I need to be witty? Should I bring snacks? Or will they bring their own?

08.22 p.m. — Picked up where I left off on *Leaves of Grass* by Walt Whitman. It is a cheap copy with an even cheaper cover bearing a stock photo of a waterfall or some shit. It was bothering me too much so I ripped the cover off, along with it, some bitch mother's inscription to her daughter.

08.40 p.m. — Spoke to Von Godi again on the telephone. He has given me special instructions not to show up to the bar until after he and the girl have arrived. Ah ha! Wingman. I understand now. We are going to ambush the girl. I am not comfortable with this. I really think he should just try talking to her first. I want a taco.

10.32 p.m. — Thomas, the artist, and Ryan came by on their way to the bar.
"I should probably eat something first," I said.
"They have a drink called a pancake shot."
"Pardon me?"
"A pancake shot," Ryan continued. "I don't know what's in it, but the booze tastes just like pancakes and maple syrup."

10.34 p.m. — Heading to the bar with Thomas the artist and Ryan for a well-balanced breakfast.

WEDNESDAY

04.58 p.m. — My hands are beginning to shake all the time now. Tremors just go with the territory. On the plus side, I have become pretty handy with a saltshaker, and masturbation is almost effortless.

06.40 p.m. — Had a bottle of red with a side of Hemingway for lunch. I drank and read on my bed, at my desk, in the bathtub, then back in my bed again. A moveable feast indeed. By the way, never read *The Odyssey* while you're hungry.

09.30 p.m. — I need to get out and get some form of exercise other than masturbation. I think I'll walk to the bar tonight.

THURSDAY

03.30 p.m. — Woke up, drained what was left of the bottle of red that I slept next to, then walked down to a local cafe for an actual food-based breakfast. Saw Byron and his girlfriend and we decided to arrange another dinner party at a mutual friend's home. I wonder if the witch doctor will be there.

05.45 p.m. — New bottle. Continued working on one of my short stories, titled *Madd Man*, that no one will ever read, and another novella that I've begun writing.

11.40 p.m. — I am stoned and drunk. I think I'll stop for the evening. Typewriter seems to be keeping Moscow and Amos awake.

SATURDAY

06.58 p.m. — Stepped out onto my back balcony for a cigarette and noticed one of my downstairs neighbors squatting down in the drainage ditch, burning a small pile of documents or something.

"Will you be fucking careful with that shit please," I barked at him. "This whole goddamn town is made of wood and caulked with douchebags. The whole place could go up in flames at any minute as it is."

SUNDAY

04.01 p.m. — I am a creature of habit. (Except when I'm not.) For the most part, I wake up (by no discernible schedule, though more towards mid to late afternoon), but I do not get up. I am not governed by any daily motivator, so it is rather easy to convince myself that there is no overwhelming benefit to getting out of bed, so I do not. Most days, I will not even bother to open my eyes upon my first conscious stir. I allow myself to fall back to sleep, and normally stay that way for a couple hours more. I will, however, get out of bed the second time I wake up. I will light the day's first cigarette, and either make coffee, or open a bottle of wine. Normally, I try to lean towards coffee first. (I try.) So, after I open the bottle, I will have two or three cigarettes and about three or four 'cups of coffee' before I decide to get dressed. (Use word "dressed" loosely.) I will then sit outside in the shade with my cats and read for a few hours, (or in the winter, next to the window by the bed) or busy myself with some unimportant task. By then, it is normally starting to get dark. If I have finished my first bottle by then, (I usually have) I will pop open a new one, light another cigarette and sit down in front of my typewriter. The typing will usually start pretty soon. And so my day will continue, punctuated only by a quick meal at a cafe, to read for a bit, or to go buy 'coffee' and cigarettes. Evenings are headlined by the bar, and capped off by either more writing, or stuffing my face with a TV dinner and passing out on top of a small, semi-retarded cat. That is it.

I am a writer.

Hear me roar.

MONDAY
08.35 p.m. — Finished the first 'final' draft of my novella. Heading to the bar to celebrate my literary greatness.

TUESDAY
03.24 a.m. — Thomas, the artist, and I decided to go bar hopping. That guy can drink. But so can I. We started getting a little wobbly after the fourth bar, and I am pretty sure I almost killed us by driving on the wrong side of the street. We made it back to his studio and smoked a joint while he showed me some of his latest work. After about an hour, I took my leave and captained my swervy ship back home, blaring Mozart the whole way. After I surprisingly made it back home, my head started spinning and I passed out on my kitchen floor with my back door

open to the sound of the song *Stayin' Alive* coming from a house party nearby. I am going to make a wild extrapolation and say I was heading to my back balcony to dance, and just didn't quite make it.

03.40 p.m. — A bottle of red while I sort through some 35mm proof sheets of some photos I took in New York, Paris and Norway. Some of the shots look really good. Goddamn, that bottle went fast.

03.55 p.m. — New bottle.

09.00 p.m. — Am I socially awkward in an alienating way? I mean, I know I am not exactly a 'ten' as they say, (a four or five is more likely) but is that it? Do I do weird things without noticing? Do I unwittingly verbalize my thoughts? Does this person now know that I think she is dressed like a bitch, and that it matches her personality? Or something more physical perhaps. Am I the guy who is always doing weird things with his jaw, like repetitive gnawing motions or something? Maybe I smell. Maybe I smile too much, revealing my pirate teeth. Maybe I don't smile enough.

WEDNESDAY
07.00 p.m.— New bottle. New poem.
Here is the womb of life,
the death of our mind's night.
New eyes that long to open,
new wings that spread to flight.
A birth of new vocation,

souls shed ephemeral strife,
the heart bestows new purpose,
in this, the womb of life.
No god, no king,
nor roots hold greater might,
each one so frail and barren,
in this new guiding light.
For here stands love,
its meaning right,
here is the womb of life.

FRIDAY
04.19 p.m. — Von Godi has requested my assistance in the quality control and product evaluation of a bottle of champagne and a bottle of vodka. I am honored to be a part of this study and will take my duties very seriously.

08.40 p.m. — First stage of our study is complete, but we need to continue our work. There is a bar not far from here that presently has a happy hour in effect, and we have a few more tests we need to conduct with similar fluids in different formulas. It would be bad science not to, really.
09.40 p.m. — We only had time to evaluate about six cocktails each before we were asked to leave. (I'll never reveal why.) Be that as it may, we're still not convinced of our findings. We shall return to Von Godi's house and continue. Our work must not be interfered with.

11.32 p.m. — One bottle of bourbon depleted.

SATURDAY

01.10 a.m. — One bottle of Irish whiskey depleted.

03.20 a.m. — We have discovered another bottle of vodka and acquired a six pack of cheap beer. There is a party going on down the street and professor Von Godi and I have resolved to making contact with this group of fellow scientists and combining our research with theirs.

06.12 a.m. — Study complete. Not sure what notable conclusion we arrived at, but all I remember are a few foggy scenes involving a bottle of vodka, a bottle of bourbon and two other bottles. (Compounds still unidentified.) I remember the other researchers had a bar in their backyard. (They had proper funding.) I remember appointing myself bartender and pouring shots for everyone. I remember one researcher vomiting next to the bar. I remember some obnoxious guy with a guitar. (Everyone secretly wishes 'that guy' would shut the fuck up.) I remember a second researcher vomiting. I remember (shortly after Von Godi lost most of his motor functions), paying a researcher ten bucks to help me carry Von Godi back down the street to his house. I remember waking up an unknown length of time later on Von Godi's living room floor in a pool of my own vomit. (I hope it was mine.) I remember Von Godi waking up a short time later, proclaiming that someone had stolen his pants. (He never found them.) Finally, I remember, shortly after collecting ourselves, heading to the bar for a few drinks.

09.40 p.m. — New bottle.

11.11 p.m. — So I am now a co-founding member of a community gardening project, along with my neighbor, Ryan. Stay off the sauce kids. It'll make you do some strange things.

FRIDAY
11.00 p.m. — Trying to look over some notes for a rather large work I am going to write. Should be around forty to fifty chapters. I am hoping these notes, and *The Firebird Suite* will get my brain going. I may need to pull a cork and lubricate the gears.

11.40 p.m. — Cork pulled. Lubricating gears.

SATURDAY
03.01 a.m. — Shit. Too much lubrication. I slipped and fell down.

TUESDAY
02.30 p.m. — Managed to get my hands on an old copy of a late work by Gertrude Stein. A play titled *In Savoy* which was almost the last thing she wrote.

THURSDAY
02.02 a.m. — There were these three young girls at the bar tonight, and not one of them looked a day over twenty-one. They seemed to be learning how to drink. (I wish they would go to a kid's bar for that sort of thing.) One of the girls happened to catch one of the bartenders and myself laughing at them a little. She sent us a sort of

sneering 'fuck you' look while her face was still disabled from the shot she took. (Which honestly just made it funnier) Expect those types of looks and laughs from veteran drunks, kid.

03.26 a.m. — There is this homeless guy who has been camping out in the small city aqueduct behind my building for the last couple of days. I made him a huge sandwich and packed him a paper bag full of other things I thought he could use, like other food, a spare lighter, a couple packs of smokes and a twenty-dollar bill. He claimed to be a poet himself, then proceeded to recite the same poem to me, twice. I lit a joint for us to smoke while we conversed, and he claimed to know two friends of mine. After he started getting a little high, he confessed that he was actually on the run from the police for murder. I then thanked him for a lovely evening. He told me he loved me. I then walked around to the street side of my building so my new lover couldn't see which door I went into.

03.40 a.m. — New bottle.

06.40 a.m. — You know that stage in a young girl's life when her body begins to develop a protective wall in her stomach (or whatever) that will serve as a custodial environment for any potential baby? I think that is starting to happen in my stomach. My guts are beginning to construct a protective barrier for the gallons of booze my stomach is being forced to carry around.

03.20 p.m. — Started reading *Lolita* by Vladimir Nabokov.

06.14 p.m. — Walked out onto my front balcony to the echoing bangs of a fireworks display being held at the university a few blocks away, honoring the year's graduating class. The streets are littered with intoxicated college students. I must remember not to step in anything if I go for a walk this evening. Dog shit. Student vomit. Student shit. A nasty, steaming pile of broken dreams left behind by the ones that failed.

We come to you with bright shining faces
and wounds still fresh from the womb,
grabbing at anything cool.
We pretend to be naked
and drink from the fountain of delusion.
The fountain of truth is too cold to swallow.
The protective gates of benevolence have been opened,
and with hedonistic indoctrination
we crash into the streets
in search of instantaneous wine
and blind absolution.
We dine on chaos and pay with inherited coin.
We adore our futile reflections in mirrors,
scoffing at inevitability.
We bathe in drive-thru lust.
We crave the warmth of a cold pillow.
We will always be hungry.
We will always want a better place to play.

WEDNESDAY
09.40 p.m.— Finished reading *Lolita*. Jesus Christ, I need a drink. Maybe three.

SATURDAY
04.19 p.m. — For about the past twenty minutes, there have been two ambulances meandering around my end of the block, like they are looking for something. I highly doubt, however, that they have anything to do with that disheveled young woman who has neatly tucked herself under the brown station wagon, covering her eyes with her hands to make herself invisible.

05.51 p.m. — There is this college band who is doing their band practice in a (very) nearby house. You could tell they were really trying. A random neighbor here and there would give a quick cheer or clap. I am a lover of music and the arts. I wanted to give them some encouragement as well. But I am also an honest man, so I wanted it to be sincere. So, I shouted the most honest thing I could think of.

SUNDAY
06.02 p.m. — In the city center, there are a few nice places with benches that I like to sit and read or write. There weren't many people about this afternoon, so it was nice and quiet. After about forty minutes, this girl in her early twenties came and sat down next to me. She was very pretty with a bright smile and warm brown eyes.

"What are you writing, if you don't mind me asking? You had a very deep, consumed look on your face."

I wasn't really in the mood for conversation.

"Poetry. I write poetry."

"Oh wow! I love poets." She smiled invitingly.

Inching closer, she asked, "Could you write me a poem, maybe?"

"Sure thing," I said, licking the tip of my pen and turning to a blank page. She sat there ever so patiently, watching people walk by, watching me scribble, and occasionally peeking her ponytailed head over to try and have a look at what I was writing. I finished and folded it, lit a cigarette, handed it to her and walked away, never looking back.

Oh, my little apple sweet hummingbird.
The many ways I could eternally brand my memory into your moistest of dreams.
The ways I could endearingly massage your soft thighs with my tongue, and as a newly sprouting tulip bud tenderly weaves through its young enveloping petals, part your two warm, wet, butterscotch lips, and caress the depths of your most taboo desires.
I could thrust into you like a train with gushing waves of carnal lust. The flavor of exploding stars rocketing from your honey pot to the most love starved chambers of your throbbing heart, crashing the ideas of love and lust together with such passionate force, not even god could tell them apart.

11.57 p.m. — Moscow just died. Thirty minutes ago. In my arms.

Fuck cancer.

11.58 p.m. — New bottle.

MONDAY
12.20 a.m. — New bottle.
12.58 a.m. — New bottle.
01.25 a.m. — New bottle.
01.51 a.m. — New bottle.
02.22 a.m. — New bottle.
02.59 a.m. — New bottle.

FRIDAY
04.10 p.m. — A knock at the door. I didn't answer it right away, as I was not expecting anyone. I am not exactly the 'host company' type. I looked through the peephole. It was some young college girl. I lit a cigarette and sat down on my bed, hoping she would go away. Another knock. I looked through the peephole again. Same girl. She isn't going away. She is just standing there at my door, writing in a notepad. I finally opened the door.

"Oh hi!" she chirped, popping up from her notepad like a bubbly whack-a-mole.

"I'm Nicole!" she continued, extending her hand.

"Can I help you, miss?"

"Oh yeah, sorry. I blanked for a second there. I just wanted to invite you to a house show at the address behind your building," she said, adjusting her top to show her breasts a little more.

"Okay."

"It shouldn't run too late, but it'll be a good time. Will I get to see you there?"

"We'll see," I said, closing the door in her face.

No. You won't see me at your party. These college kids invite you (as neighbors) not because they have the slightest interest in knowing you. They only try and make you feel invited because they don't want you calling the cops on their party. Sorry sweetheart. You can take your perfect young tits and shove them up your perfect young ass. I have shit to do.

SATURDAY

08.10 p.m. — I just had sex! Haha. Just kidding. Goddamn it.

08.11 p.m. — Fuck it. I'm going to the bar.

An evening at the bar.

*Soft amber lights
shining down on rich wooden altars,
warm refrains and hearty,
clamorous greetings
from one comrade to another.
The shared connectivity
that draws these humans
into debaucherous,
celebratory ritual,
gives a fervent consoling hug
of understanding to its
faithful participants.
We gather at this altar
of consumption to partake,
to swig and swill,
toast and cheers,
to sip and guzzle,
to renew, to forget and celebrate.
And sometimes,
to mourn our pitiful lives
in the hopes of discovering
that we are not alone,
or to find some great exit
from our common pains.
How dutifully we maintain
our depressions with liquid resolve.
How willingly we kiss our sorrows
with mocking celebration.
What a tragic comedy we are.*

#

SATURDAY
08.12 p.m. — I'm in love. And guess what. She's a red. New bottle.

01.32 a.m. — There is a party going down at the house behind my building. I can't see them due to the trees that line the canal between our dwellings, but through the music I can make out random conversations. One person is barking at another to find a Ouija board so they can talk to Andy Kaufman. Who the fuck are these people?

04. 10 p.m. — I accidentally threw my car keys in the dumpster. Jumping inside one of those things is an experience everyone should be subject to. Not just once, but every so often. To remind you. You are expendable and can be reduced to the gutters in an instant. And people will leave you there.

WEDNESDAY
05.10 p.m. — A bottle of Bluebird wine and the classical work of Rossini, *The Barber of Seville* for breakfast.

SATURDAY
04.40 p.m. — Helping Von Godi move into his new place. We performed a good portion of the task under the influence of booze and valium, then capped off the evening's labor by shooting fireworks at unsuspecting rednecks while screaming, "Vive la France" in honor of Bastille Day.

SUNDAY
07.02 p.m. — New bottle.

10.11 p.m. — Met up with Dylan, a writer friend of mine who works part time as a bartender at one of my local holes. He wanted me to look over his latest story. Normally, he writes science fiction, which personally I'm not in to. So I was proud to see that his latest was nothing of the sort. He had gotten drunk a few nights prior, and with pen in hand, proceeded to bleed all over his notebook. I couldn't have been prouder of him.

FRIDAY
01.10 a.m. — Met up with a couple of university students that I am acquainted with (for reasons I can't presently remember). One of which, Alex, a philosophy major, persistently tries to convince me to invest in the purchase of a submarine with him, with the goal of becoming a sovereign nation in perpetual transit and engaging in piracy. (Yes. This is a real person, with a degree.)

SATURDAY
11.20 p.m. — Bar hopping with Von Godi for his birthday, along with roughly five members of Von Godi's artist collective. I spent over twenty minutes in the bathroom at one point, trying to inflate an inflatable sheep sex toy that I had purchased from the condom machine. I was very drunk, so I had to keep taking breaks from getting light-headed. I thought it would be at least mildly entertaining to bounce the sheep around the bar

like a beach ball. The people waiting in line when I finally came out of the bathroom, huffing and puffing with the sheep under my arm thought it was funny for different reasons. Goddamn it.

MONDAY
03.10 p.m. — They are repairing the water main on my end of the block. It breaks about once a month. I am getting drunk and watching all the pissy, whiny people cuss and flail their fists because they have to turn around and make a four-minute detour due to the street closure. Really, how dare these city workers use the people's tax money to fix public roads without consulting everyone's personal schedule first.

TUESDAY
09.50 p.m. — Making corrections to a short story I wrote a while back. Nothing big. Just spelling and punctuation that I missed out of exhaustion.

"Yeah, I saw all those mistakes when I read the final draft," Von Godi said.

"Why didn't you tell me before I went to print with it?"

"You told me not to point out mistakes. I think you threatened me if I did, actually."

10.15 p.m. — New bottle. New poem.

WEDNESDAY
09.09 p.m. — My building has mice now. That should keep my cat busy.

FRIDAY
04.50 p.m. — Finished reading, *Seven Years in Tibet*.

05.31 p.m. — Killed the eight cockroaches living in my coffee pot. There. Now I can make coffee.

SUNDAY
02.20 a.m. — Attempting to read Faulkner under the influence of two bottles of red and two bottles of cheap vodka. *As I Lay Dying* is beginning to take on a whole new meaning.

THURSDAY
07.02 p.m. — Went to a party at Von Godi's. It was a celebration of the recent achievements of the artist collective that Von Godi is involved in. I only had the chance to swallow up a half a bottle of bourbon before this twenty-two-year-old girl became a bit too intoxicated and begged me for a ride home. I didn't realize she meant my home, until we were at her house. (Damn it.)

SUNDAY
09.50 p.m. — Completed *As I Lay Dying* and started *The Man Who Laughs* by Victor Hugo, with a side of le rouge.

11.31 p.m. — Stepped out onto my back balcony for a cigarette, when one of the new tenants from the house next door to my building came stumbling around the corner with her housemate. She was babbling something about a fear she has of homeless people squatting in her attic. They appeared to be inspecting the house, looking for any space that someone could crawl in near the roof. It was too dark for them to see me, however. I think I know how I'll be entertaining myself over the coming months. New bottle.

MONDAY

02.15 p.m. — Getting drunk on red and watching the day walkers drone past from the window. It has been raining for over a week straight.

11.40 p.m. — Amos and I were just engaged in combat with a raccoon. The thieving, gypsy cunt had snuck into my kitchen in attempts to steal Amos' food. Amos started making quite the ruckus, and I came running in with a bottle of red in one hand, and a Zulu spear in the other that I had acquired somehow while I was in South Africa. There was still wine in the bottle, so I couldn't rightly throw that at him. Taking a heavy breasted chug, I lunged the spear at the raccoon, missing him and wounding my wine rack. I took another great chug, finishing the bottle's contents and threw it at the fat little bastard's head. It then ran towards Amos, (who jumped about six feet in the air to avoid the vermin's charge) before escaping through the back door. Ambitious little prick.

TUESDAY

12.19 a.m. — I just realized that I only have $2.31 to my name. Not sure how long it's been like that. At least I have zero debt, which is more than I can say for over eighty percent of the country.

03.04 a.m. — I wonder if people think I am secretly a cross-dresser. I drink so much wine, my lips are always a reddish purple. Looks like lipstick that I forgot to wash off.

WEDNESDAY
07.19 p.m. — You know why history repeats itself? Because people refuse to learn from it.
We spent today singing of tomorrow,
but tomorrow never came.
With naive hearts we wrote undying
love songs to transient, deciduous souls.
We mockingly sat deaf
at the foot of wise men's lectures,
while we barked mute revolution.
Brains thrashed in dormant bodies,
and we celebrated enlightened states of nothingness.
We played with our lives
the way a child plays with a gun,
and we spent today singing of tomorrow,
but tomorrow never came.

THURSDAY
07.20 p.m. — New bottle. Mailed off two more poems to a literary magazine.

FRIDAY
04.00 p.m. — I don't think I own a single pair of socks that don't have holes in them. Doesn't seem to pose any remarkable drawbacks, so no sense in buying new ones.

SATURDAY

05.59 p.m. — Another rainy morning. Another red breakfast.

07.20 p.m. — Von Godi has loaned me twenty dollars. That will get me another two or three bottles of red, and a couple packs of cigarettes. I owe him money now. I don't like that. I haven't owed anyone anything since that strip club in Valletta, Malta over a decade ago. And that wasn't even my debt. The French kid I was with got too drunk and forgot how many dances he got, despite my warnings to pay attention.

"Look, Frenchie. Fucking pay attention while you're in this place. Got it?"
"Oui, monsieur."
"If these girls know you're drunk, they'll try to take you for every dime you've got. Understand?"
"Oui, monsieur."
"This is an important thing we're doing here, Frenchie. We're helping this poor island economy and putting food on people's tables."
"Oui, monsieur."

10.11 p.m. — Bought three cheap bottles of red and three packs of cigarettes. While walking back from the corner store, I came to a rather unpleasant realization. I'm going to have to get a fucking job.

10.40 p.m. — New bottle. New poem.

The dark and quiet hours of closed bars
and vacant cars,
swaying, staggering silhouettes
and figures on distance street corners
and alleyways.
Broken bottles, vomit puddles
and vultures in blue uniforms picking off the strays.
Dope dealers and daddy's little girl
peddling and dancing under the warm
orange glow of street lamps.
Traffic signals direct absent traffic.
A ghost town alive with shadows
that cruise around like heroin through the veins.
Here in the dingy downtown bowels of midnight,
there are only fallen stars and distant dreams.

TUESDAY
01.02 a.m. — I'm having trouble remembering when I last paid rent. Come to think of it, I'm not even entirely sure who my landlord is, or that I have ever met him. He could be anybody. I was pretty drunk when I crash-landed in this hovel.

WEDNESDAY
11.58 p.m. — Hit and run at the corner. The guy was drunk and almost took out a late-night construction crew that was working on the sewer, before plowing his car into a parked vehicle. The guys from the construction crew helped him out of his car and he took off 'running'. He fell down a couple of times in the process. Police found him hiding in the drainage ditch behind my building.

THURSDAY

01.03 a.m. — New poem.
Every city,
every town,
is like a madman
with a split personality.
Resigned,
docile,
seemingly typical
throughout his day.
But between the hours
of eleven p.m.
and four a.m.,
the curtain falls
on his paid masquerade.
He rips his face off.
He is a freed maniac.
A drunken,
biting,
clawing psychopath.
Fighting.
Fucking.
Guzzling.
His true self.

02.02 a.m. — City bus just clipped the side of a parked car on the corner. Bus driver didn't run. His supervisor showed up and started yelling at him. Then the passengers started yelling at him. Then the owner of the car he hit got in on the action. The driver just sat there with his head in his hands, saying nothing, submissively taking in every curse and insult for minimum wage.

SATURDAY
02.35 a.m. — One of my neighbors lost his job as a teaching assistant at the university. Apparently, they caught him with some questionable pornography. Now he is drunk and pissed, smashing things in his apartment (which always smells like body odor and rotting semen when you walk by his door) and stomping back and forth across our shared second floor balcony. If he doesn't pipe the fuck down, I am going to step outside and throw him over the railing.

SUNDAY
09.49 p.m. — Finished reading *The Man Who Laughs* by Victor Hugo. Started reading *The Picture of Dorian Gray* by the great Oscar Wilde. Mailed off two more poems.

MONDAY
09.01 a.m. — Drained a bottle of red while I get dressed. I am going to have to catch the bus if I'm going to make it to the Goodwill for a job interview I got out of yesterday's paper. I don't know how this is going to pan out.

09.40 a.m. — City trains and buses are captivating environments. A microcosmos of the clinically insane. Migrant half families, paramedics tending to imaginary ailments of residentially challenged NASCAR drivers, a cellist. I sat next to a man with neck tattoos who had likely been sleeping in that seat for the past forty-eight hours. He claimed to be a very important butler in Cleveland. His eyes grew to the size of silver dollars when I pulled my flask of bourbon from my coat pocket. "Down boy."

10.10 a.m. — I have (sort of) been greeted, inducted, toured and name badged by big-legged Bertha, the manager of the local Goodwill. I am taking covert swigs from my flask when she isn't condescending directly at me. This place smells like urine and floor cleaner.

10.40 a.m. — I was instructed to "clean the toy rack", which is code for the box of chickenpox coated toy cars, cap guns and leftovers of various snot stained Halloween costumes.

10.42 a.m. — Smoking cigarettes and taking shots behind the building. I'm not sticking my hands in that fucking box.

10.58 a.m. — Instructed to help customers. This place has no screening process, whatsoever. Anyone can work here. "Where are the coats, you ask? Why, they're right down that aisle, next to the used children's panties and semi-functional toasters."

01.48 p.m. — There's this kid who works here named Connor (and by work, I mean community service), who gets bored when there are no customers, and instantly becomes annoying. He likes to do things like jump out

from behind clothing racks and shoot me with one of those toy guns that shoot big foam balls. But since nobody ever includes the balls when they donate the toy gun, it just shoots puffs of air and germs.
"I shot you! Haha! You have pink eye now."

05.00 p.m. — Punched out for the day. Borrowed thirty bucks against my next check from big-legged Bertha. I definitely need a drink.

06.01 p.m. — Tucked up in the warm embrace of my humble hovel. Continuing to read *The Picture of Dorian Gray* by the great Oscar Wilde.

08.15 p.m. — Heading to the bar. That thirty dollars should keep the tap flowing for a few hours.

09.40 p.m. — Met up with Von Godi and Mr James, who is a manager for some famous rock band from Los Angeles. Two bottles of tequila later (I despise tequila), James appointed himself doorman to a local bar and began checking people's ID. After being asked to leave by the real doorman, we proceeded to the next place we'd get booted from, the twenty-four-hour diner. They didn't seem to appreciate our creativity in trying to sell the table mayo to other customers to pay for our meal.

11.15 p.m. — New poem.
I'm a poet.
I have something to say.
It's powerful,

it's beautiful,
it's sexy.
I don't care about meter or rhyme.
I don't care about beat or form.
I'm a poet.
I have something to say.
I just don't know how to say it yet.
But it's there.
I can feel it.
It's there,
clawing at the inside of my chest.
It has pushed through the meat between my ribs,
and is just underneath my skin,
deforming me.
I can almost see it when I turn out the light.
Its spiny legs start to crawl out of my mouth,
then my tongue moves and scares it away.
I can feel it coming back just now.
Don't move.
Don't make a sound.
It will come if you just shut up.
You'll see.
You won't be able to look away.
It's as big as a god.
It has wings and it will fly around the world
and no one will be able to stop it.
I just have to think about it a little longer.
It will come.
It will make you love me.
It will make the world love me.
It will make you put down your gun.

It could make you pick one up.
The worms are following me.
They know it's coming.
When it comes, it will burst out of me,
and take everything inside me with it.
The empty shell of what will be left
will fall to the earth,
and these squirming beasts will eat
the hollow cadaver.
They will consume all evidence
that the old me ever existed.

TUESDAY

09.40 a.m. — Hungover on the bus. Downing bourbon to try and make my head stop pounding. This is going to be a long day.

10.00 a.m. — Punched in and walked out back for a cigarette. It is too goddamn early for customers, or service.

10.40 a.m. — Still sitting out back behind the dumpster, smoking cigarettes and puking, and trying to finish *The Picture of Dorian Gray*. Still don't feel like going out onto the floor yet.

11.39 a.m. — Dragged myself back inside to clock out for lunch. Walked across the street to the liquor store for a fifth of bourbon and a taco.

12.39 p.m. — Clocked back in while big-legged Bertha explained to me that lunch is thirty minutes, not an hour.

12.42 p.m. — Walked out on the sales floor and saw Connor sniffing the old sport coats on the racks. He liked to think that he could tell which ones were donated as a result of someone dying, versus someone simply cleaning out an old closet. If the coat smells like mothballs and old books, the owner is dead. If it smells like between the cushions of your couch, then the owner is still alive.

12.45 p.m. — "He's fucking weird." Penny was her name. She couldn't have been more than twenty-one. She had these beautiful blue, apple leaf shaped eyes and a small, silver nose ring. She was talking about Connor. I hadn't even noticed she was standing right next to me. I liked her immediately when she asked me if she could have a swig of whatever it was I was reeking of.

01.30 p.m. — Penny and I just got fired after big-legged Bertha caught us hiding in the little plastic kids' playhouse, passing the flask back and forth.

02.10 p.m. — Getting drunk on the bus with Penny.

03.02 p.m. — Getting drunk at my place with Penny.

03.20 p.m. — Electricity got cut off while Penny and I were about to defeat our second four-dollar bottle of red.
"You have wine, books and candles. What do you need electricity for?"
I think I may be falling in love with this girl.

03.33 p.m. — Penny pulled out this little travel chessboard she carries around with her. We played for an hour or so before she started looking through my books.

"You read a lot, huh."

"Maybe. Maybe I'm just trying to look smart."

"No. The genres are too specific. You read. A lot."

Then she came across a mess of various poems I had in a pile on my desk.

"You write poetry?"

After answering in the affirmative, she asked me if I could write her one, and if the way those eyes were twinkling at me was any indication of where this conversation was headed, I'd have written her an epic right then and there. So, I got to work.

I massage her thighs with a pen.
I ignite like sulfur,
that beautiful gift that makes her a woman,
with the poetry of my tongue.
She lays there, on the pages of my notebook.
Her fresh, inviting young body,
throbbing and hungry,
to feel the warm ink of my desire,
dripping down her flowering curves.
The tip of love's pen,
caressing the velvet pages of her youthful skin,
scribing passionately a poem of lust,
of desire fulfilled.
Words only she can read.
Words only he can write.

04.58 p.m. — I open another bottle and hand her the poem. She pulls my hand and the poem and rubs them across her lap. I push the poem down her panties. We make love.

WEDNESDAY
03.45 p.m. — The London Symphony Orchestra, a joint and chapter fifteen of *The Picture of Dorian Gray*.

07.20 p.m. — Found my old flask behind my Thomas Home phonograph. Still three-quarters full of bourbon. That should keep my engine running for a bit.

11.01 p.m. — Started writing out the beginnings of another small novella.

THURSDAY
03.10 a.m. — Electricity is still off. Took a bucket bath and drank myself to sleep.

SATURDAY
02.03 p.m. — Walked a few blocks to a pet store in another attempt at finding a job. They hired me on the spot and had me start right away. Within the first forty minutes, I got bit by a baby snake, I was sexually assaulted by an English bulldog, got called an asshole by a smart-assed parrot and watched a goldfish get murdered by a snot-nosed nine year old.

I quit.

SUNDAY
01.01 a.m. — Finished reading *The Picture of Dorian Gray*. My favorite line in the book. *Life always has poppies in her hands.*

04.21 p.m. — Borrowed another twenty from Von Godi. Bought three more bottles of red. I killed one as I walked over to the city utilities office to apply for a grace extension to get my lights turned back on.

05.40 p.m. — Walked to the corner store for bread, bologna and cheese. Stopped by the bookstore and bought a cheap, fifty cent copy of *The Count of Monte Cristo*. $2.80 left over.

09.40 p.m. — Completed the first rough draft of my novella and my last two bottles of wine. Hear Wolfgang roar.

10.14 p.m. — Heading to the bar. Let's see how far this $2.80 will take me down the tap.

10.23 p.m. — Took my usual stool at my favorite hole and laid my crumpled offerings on the bar.
 "Put your money away, Wolf. What are you having?"
 They let me drink my fill. It's good to have friends. Discussed economic colonialism, flat tires and cocaine prices (adjusted for inflation).

TUESDAY
12.58 a.m. — Found a ten-dollar bill on the sidewalk as I

was walking (use term loosely) home. 'Walking' back to the bar.

04.19 a.m. — There is no exclamation mark on my 1936 Royal Standard. I guess things weren't very exciting at the Royal factory back then.

08.03 p.m. — Getting drunk on bourbon at Von Godi's house. His neighbors across the street have this little cut-out of a kid, which I assume is supposed to serve as a warning sign of some sort to inspire passing motorists to be more conscientious about their speed. We have reconditioned said cut-out by taping a large kitchen knife to its hand and have placed a dead raccoon at its feet. Now that, will send a warning.

10.40 p.m. — Just ran into 'The Colonel' on my way into the bar. The Colonel is a retired military officer who had gone insane (literally) some years back. He was, at the time of my running into him, drunk, naked and brandishing his Marine Corps sword. It was good to see him still doing well.

WEDNESDAY
01.10 a.m. — Tried working on the novella at the bar, but the wildlife that was coming in off the street was far too distracting, so I just got drunk instead. Perhaps if they played classical music, I could focus there a little better. Does this exist anywhere? A dive bar that plays Mendelssohn instead of Eric Clapton?

02.45 a.m. — Penny saw me stumbling away from a taco stand on my way home from the bar and picked me up. I still had a few pulls of bourbon left in my flask, so we sat in her car in a grocery store parking lot, finishing it off. A rather heated argument between a prostitute and her john provided a bit of entertainment. The prostitute cursed and threw bottles at the guy for a good ten minutes before he was able to get away.

"Well, that's it," I said as I took the final swig of bourbon. "I'm broke."

Penny turned and looked at me with those two beautiful blue eyes as if to say, you poor thing. She climbed over to the passenger seat, sat on my lap, unzipped my pants and made love to me. After, I lit us both a cigarette and, still sitting on top of me, and taking a long slow drag as she leaned back against the dashboard she said, "I can probably get you a job at 7Eleven."

THURSDAY
04.15 p.m. — Penny brought me a few bottles of cheap red, and a few bottles of various bourbons and whiskeys so I could make a couple of my favorite cocktails. I think I may be falling in love. Not because she buys me booze. (although...)

08.06 p.m. — Luca Marenzio's *Leggiadare Ninfe*, a joint and *The Count of Monte Cristo* for dinner.

02.00 p.m. — First day of work at 7Eleven. If you've never worked at a corner store, you've missed out on something profound. Aside from getting paid by a business that has little to no expectations of you, you get to experience a clientele of unparalleled diversity. On the downside, you have to interact with each and every one of them. This should be, something.

04.33 p.m. — I've discovered that I hate the spring-loaded coffee cup dispenser. Every time I try to pull a coffee cup out, the mechanism overreacts and launches cups out all over the floor like a goddamn jack-in-the-box.

05.40 p.m. — "What drinks you got that are free?" the douchebag asked.
"There's a water spigot on the side of the building."
"No, I mean like slurpies n' shit."
"There's a water spigot on the side of the building."
"Come on, man. You ain't going to sell all the slurpies anyway."
"Water spigot."
"Fuck you then. I'll take my business elsewhere."

10.00 p.m. — Clocked out. I think I can actually do this.

10.30 p.m. — New bottle. Knocked out two more chapters of *The Count of Monte Cristo*, then scribbled out a new poem.

As two flowers swaying on a hill,
standing side by side,
who can only touch and feel their kiss,
when the right wind blows their way.

*Each momentary tickle
of your tender little petals,
send waves of joy and love carefree,
before the winds pull you away from me.
And I can only wait and marvel,
at your colors in the sun,
until that bittersweet wind
should come and blow,
our longing blossoms together again.
So close but yet so far.*

SATURDAY

02.43 a.m. — DUI stop in front of my building. A boyfriend and a girlfriend. Girlfriend was driving. Girlfriend is being given a sobriety test. Girlfriend is getting put in handcuffs. Girlfriend is crying. Boyfriend is trying to watch it all in the side mirror. It was pretty comical watching the fat cop demonstrate the heel-to-toe walk. He waddled like a chubby duck. His partner, clearly disinterested, stood in the background while half-heartedly mimicking the test out of boredom.

01.30 p.m. — Bottle of le rouge and Rachmaninoff Symphony No.1 for breakfast. Walking to 7Eleven for my second day of work.

02.00 p.m. — Clocked in. Away we go.

07.07 p.m. — There is a guy who comes in twice a day, walks over to the slurpie machine, raises his arms in a gesture of religious praise and yells, "Black Jesus is here!" This peculiar event would make more sense if the guy were actually black.

08.01 p.m. — Tuned the store radio to a classical station. If I had to listen to one more Journey song, I was going to go out back and fling myself into the dumpster.

08.30 p.m. — Cigarette break. Went around the side of the store and had a drink with the homeless guy who'd set up camp there over the past two days.

"Hey, Mr 7Eleven guy. You got another one of them smokes?"

"Sure, if you can part with a couple of swigs of that vodka."

"You got it, Mr 7Eleven man. You give, I give. Who needs charity."

09.30 p.m. — A public service announcement to all of you people who steal from corner stores. If it's a privately owned family store, then don't. You're taking money from a family who works a hell of a lot harder than you do. Your fellow working man. But if it's a corporate chain, keep in mind, everything you steal or destroy, you guarantee their profit via insurance. (They get paid, and you go to jail, which on the thief's part, is ignorant and borderline retarded behavior if you ask me.) Furthermore, the employees in these places are treated like shit and make minimum wage. If it looks like we don't give a shit about you, or our job, then assume we don't and conduct yourselves accordingly. And assume that we probably don't give a shit that you just pocketed a goddamn bag of Skittles. Just know though, we saw you take it. We always see it.

10.00 p.m. — Clocked out. Bought three cheap bottles of red and walked home.

10.42 p.m. — You know what the most powerful word in the world is?
Hunger.

11.39 p.m. — Penny is working on her university government homework here at my place by candlelight.
"Name a group of people in this country that have had their civil rights violated, that aren't black."
Easy enough to answer. Taking a healthy chug of red, I replied, "Fucking everyone. The natives, the Irish, Mexicans, the Chinese, the Vietnamese, Jews, gays, communists. Everyone. This is a nation of hate and discontent. If you have any particular viewpoint or are different than any given asshole on the street, then guaranteed, there's someone out there who hates you for it."

MONDAY
02.00 p.m. — Clocked in for work.

02.01 p.m. — Cigarette break.

02.46 p.m. — Cigarette break over.

04.50 p.m. — There's this guy who comes in almost every day for two six packs of beer. I hate having to ring him up. He smells like a public bathroom trash can. He always (always, as in every fucking time), lifts his cash to his mouth and kisses his money goodbye as he pays. A sentiment I understand completely, but his fucking mouth is always excessively wet, and there is always a disgusting string of drool clinging from his lips to the bills when he hands them to me.

04.59 p.m. — Bought a bottle of Thunderbird and went around back for a cigarette break.

07.01 p.m. — The douchebag came back.
"Can you give me a free slurpie yet?"
"No."
"Why not, man? You're just going to dump it at the end of the night anyway."
"No, we don't."
"It's just ice, sugar and food coloring."
"Then it shouldn't be hard for you to go make one yourself."
"It's not like I'm asking you for a free hotdog or gas."
"I'm surprised you haven't."
"Fuck you!"
"Fuck you."
He really wants a free slurpie.

09.20 p.m. — My co-worker just lost his shit. He told me he had to take a piss. Five minutes later, I started hearing violent screams and crashing sounds coming from the bathroom. He then kicked the bathroom door off its hinges and made a beeline for the candy rack. He grabbed two handfuls of candy bars and began throwing them at

the windows, trying to break them. I sat up on the counter and lit a cigarette. (I've no idea what's going on, but this is going to be good.) He then tackled the chip rack, knocking it over before proceeding to the coffee station where he tore open every last bag of coffee and flung the grounds all over the aisle. Then he made his way to the hotdog rollers. "Oh no, not the hotdogs. That's my dinner." While he was busy growling like a dog and smashing all the ketchup packets, I made a gallant dive to save two wieners and buns. He grabbed my arm and bit me, then ran out of the store. I went to the bathroom to wash my arm off, but he had ripped the sink off the goddamn wall. Water and broken glass were all over the floor. I don't know what he was on, but he left a syringe and a switchblade in the toilet.
I quit.

10.16 p.m. — On my walk home, I passed a flier for free psychiatric counseling that had those little tabs trimmed out at the bottom, so people could take the advertiser's contact information. All the tabs had been taken.

11.15 p.m. — New bottle. Finished reading *The Count of Monte Cristo*. Started reading *Down and Out in Paris and London* by George Orwell. Tom Waits plays *Rainbirds* on my record player.

TUESDAY
01.03 a.m.— Penny came by to do homework, while I do whatever it is that I do. Uncorked a new bottle, threw on a Francoise Hardy record and started work on the second chapter of a novella.

03.15 a.m.— Stepped out onto my front balcony for a cigarette. Tow trucks are constantly hauling off people's cars from the bars a couple blocks away. These poor bastards just went for a drink to forget about their shitty day, only to have one of these assholes steal the only way these people have to get to work in the morning, then hold it for ransom to the tune of a whole week's wages. It should be legal to take a crowbar to a tow truck driver's face. No parking zone or not.

09.02 a.m.— Woke up this morning with Penny's head snuggled on my chest, and I'm ashamed to say it gave me a warm, fuzzy feeling. She made coffee before I walked her to class. On the way, she mentioned how she heard that one of her childhood friends had just passed away in her sleep. She was only eighteen years old.

09.32 p.m.— Amos is laying on a stack of books on my desk, watching me work on my novella. His brother Moscow died a year ago. Amos saw Moscow's body about ten minutes after he died, but just stepped over Moscow as if he wasn't even there. Maybe Moscow didn't seem dead. Or, maybe Amos just accepted it as, 'that was that'. I'll never know. Penny's friend and Moscow's memory have turned a light on in an old room. Bruce, Lisa, Chris, Dustin, Tiffany, Andre, Stephen and Brian. Eight friends of mine. All dead before their nineteenth birthday.

09.44 p.m.— It has finally stopped raining. There is another storm coming tomorrow. New bottle.

04.19 p.m.— Woke up to breakfast in bed. I am going to have to start hiding a bottle under my pillow more often.

06.02 p.m.— Finished reading *Down and Out in Paris and London* by George Orwell. Started reading *Keep the Aspidistra Flying* by George Orwell.

WEDNESDAY
11.32 p.m.— Stopped by the twenty-four-hour diner on my way to the bar.

"Normally most of our customers are pretty drunk by this time of night. Nice to see you can form complete sentences."

"Drunk? Lady, I don't start getting drunk until three o'clock in the morning."

"Oh, I get it. You're one of those night people. Well, we're all out of A positive. Will coffee work?"

"Sure. And a steak and eggs as well."

"You look familiar. Weren't you in here a week or so ago, drunk with a couple of your friends, trying to sell mayonnaise to people because you couldn't pay your tab?"

"Me? No. Must have been someone else. I don't have two friends."

11.58 p.m.— Finished my lunch. As I laid my cash on the table next to the check, I noticed a little stack of hand bills that had been wedged behind the ketchup and mustard.

PARTICIPANTS NEEDED.
RESEARCH ON ALCOHOL
AND STRESS
Must be willing and able to
drink alcohol
Pays $30

Now that is my kind of research.

THURSDAY
02.32 a.m.— Closed down the bar with Penny, London Jack and Dylan. Discussed the proletariat struggle, poetry and my recent aspirations on becoming a scientist.

03.15 a.m.— Continued working on the novella.

FRIDAY
07.44 p.m.— Penny has invited me to a male strip club with her and her gay friend, Benny.
"Um, sure. Why not?"

07.48 p.m.— Leaving for the male strip club.
"I need to get gas first, Wolf. Can you cover fuel if I get your drinks?"
"You got it."

07.57 p.m.— Stopped at the 7Eleven and put a male strip club's distance worth of gas in Penny's '66 Ambassador. Next stop, booze and floppy penises.

08.30 p.m.— On the patio of the male strip club with Penny, her gay friend, Benny, and a collection of his friends, passing a couple of joints around. Among the group is a Puerto Rican who seems to be upset that he was awarded a page of children's stickers in his job's monthly employee lottery, a mother and daughter barfly combo, an old, heavy-set man in suspenders who brought corn on the cob for everyone and a fantastically flamboyant black Cuban man who offered Penny acid. The bartender poured some pretty stiff drinks. Not a bad evening.

11.40 p.m.— Driving home. Pretty drunk. Penny started throwing up. I rolled down the window and lit a cigarette to fight the smell. Penny threw up again. The smell. I started throwing up. I'm trying to drive. We're both puking all over ourselves and the car.

11.59 p.m.— I carried Penny up to my bathtub, set her in, turned on the shower and climbed in with her. We both fell asleep there, fully dressed and covered in vomit under the shower. Fortunately, I never paid the water bill so the water cut off some time in the night.

SUNDAY
05.01 p.m.— Woke up in the bathtub with a red lipstick kiss on my cheek and a bottle of red tucked under my arm, with a handwritten note that read, "Breakfast in bed." Penny is a keeper.

07.10 p.m.— I wonder what goes through the minds of

passers-by when they walk past my place and see all the wine and booze bottles that have collected on my balcony and railings.

"Oh look! That old house looks nice. Oh, and that one has a nice picket fence. And that one… oh… oh, that poor guy has problems."

11.41 p.m.— Watching my very drunk neighbor stumble down the back steps with a flashlight. He is inspecting a stack of leftover window air conditioners from our building that have been abandoned by the maintenance men.

11.44 p.m.— Now he is attempting to pick one up. He is too drunk for this type of physical activity. It's hilarious.

11.49 p.m.— He keeps falling over every time he attempts to lift one. We're on attempt number four at the moment.

11.51 p.m.— He is now attempting to carry it up the stairs. I can't watch. Going back inside and uncorking a new bottle.

11.51 ½ p.m.— (from outside) Crash, boom, thud, expletives.

FRIDAY
02.20 p.m.— End of the semester for the college students. Lots of kids walking around in their graduation robes and celebrating the end of the easiest days of their lives.

Moving trucks are all over the place, making laps around the block… driving in circles… moving the kids out and on to bigger and better disappointments.

SATURDAY
09.39 p.m.— Saw Dylan at the usual hole. He was dressed up in a collar and vest. Just got a new side job at a fancy cocktail bar.

"How you feeling there, Dylan?"

"Tired. Alarm clock went off a little earlier than I'd have liked."

"It always does. Buy you a drink?"

"That's why I'm here. What are you having?"

"I could pretty much lick whiskey off the table right about now."

"I'll have one of those as well."

I had the bartender make us both the strongest cocktail he could think of.

"Here you go fellas. First one is on the house. Not sure I made them right though."

I held the glass to the light.

"Is there booze in it?"

"Yes Wolf. Lots."

"Then you made it right."

Dylan and I both took a healthy chug.

"Dylan, you look like a fucking Chippendales dancer in that get up. Do they make you climb a pole at that place as well?"

"Every fucking job I've ever had has made me climb a pole."

"Fair enough."

"Wolf, did you know that stripper poles spin? That's how strippers do that shit. Those crazy moves and all."

"No kidding."

"Yeah. Santa Claus isn't real either, by the way."

"Well, here's to almost forty years of surviving the big illusion. Cheers, Dylan."

"Cheers."

Dylan and I drank our fill on the house. Tom Waits plays *Fumblin' With the Blues* on the jukebox.

SUNDAY
04.21 p.m. — Found a dead opossum under the front stairs of my building. Hadn't been dead long. Took a closer look and saw two tiny little legs sticking out of its pouch, kicking ever so gently. It has babies. They're still alive in there.

04.26 p.m. — Pulled out eight, tiny little baby opossums, wrapped them in a towel and put them in a bowl. They're crawling around and squeaking. Eyes aren't even open yet.

06.10 p.m. — Found a check in the mailbox for $38.20. Unclaimed wages from the Goodwill. I was so drunk when Penny and I got fired that I forgot to collect on my way out the door.

08.01 p.m. — Cashed my check at the gas station as I don't have a bank account. Heading to the bar.

MONDAY
04.19 p.m. — Young pristine couple walking down the

street, making comments on a bed frame someone threw out at the dumpster.

Boyfriend. "Look at that. It's in perfect condition. Why would someone just throw that out?"

Girlfriend. "It looks cheap and trashy."

Boyfriend. "We should get my car and come back for it."

Girlfriend. "Ew. We're not trash people. If we want new furniture, daddy will buy it for us."

06.14 p.m. — The little opossums didn't make it through the night. They were just too young and immature to be fed by anyone other than their mother.

07.44 p.m. — Finished reading *Keep the Aspidistra Flying* by George Orwell. I am out of money. I am out of wine. I am out of food. The electricity has been turned off again. Strip yourself naked. See who you really are.

TUESDAY
02.20 p.m. — Reading through the literary classifieds. One reads:
Want to spend three weeks surrounded by fall foliage, walking paths and a cool, clear river while you work on your writing? Residency plus $1,500.
Who the fuck are these people?
Another reads:
Poetry prize of $500 and two cases of beer.
Now this ad is geared towards writers.

WEDNESDAY
04.10 p.m. — Working on the novella. Penny is on the

bed in a T-shirt and panties doing homework. I turn forty years old in nine months. New bottle.

SATURDAY
08.40 p.m. — A neighbor two houses down just got carted off in an ambulance. Heart attack. I guess his thirty-eight years at the office finally paid off.

08.51 p.m. — Checked my mail to see if anyone was kind enough to send me my heart attack. No bills, but I did get an acceptance letter from a poetry magazine with a check for $1,000.

09.01 p.m. — Walking to the payphone to call Penny. No answer. Walking back home.

09.10 p.m. — Penny was parked outside my building, sitting on the trunk of her car and smoking a cigarette when I got back. Showed her the letter and the check. Heading to the bar with Penny.

SUNDAY
01.48 a.m. — Spent $480 of the check at the bar. I never knew I had so many friends.

02.10 a.m. — As Penny and I were walking back to my place, a homeless guy asked me if I had any change.
    I handed him the rest of the money from the check. Penny looked at me in astonishment.
    "Did you just…"
    "Yep."

"Okay. But why?"

"He needed change. I don't. Hopefully that changes something for him. Even if it's just for a little while."

04.00 a.m. — I am broke again. I have two bottles of red, two packs of cigarettes and enough bologna and cheese to last me a few days. I have a roof over my head, more books than I could read in two years, a very comfortable bed and a beautiful young girl laying in it, waiting for me to finish typing this. I think I am going to sleep well tonight. In the solace of poverty, your sleep isn't plagued by the prisons of cachet or stature, or delusions of grandeur, because what little you have, is all that matters. The superfluous is exposed and the external reality is smashed. The meaningful is illuminated and the internal reality is elevated. If you can afford to be poor, I highly recommend it.

Poverty is the new freedom.

Poverty is clarity.

Madd Man

Across these limitless, umber brown fields of rich farm soil that stretch out in every direction, to distances only comparable to the sapphire skies that envelope them, time and space seem to intertwine so effortlessly that they become one unstoppable force.

With the exception of the sporadic, distant farm house, dancing in the gassy waves of a heat mirage, the only landmark of describable note was a single towering row of Lombardy poplar trees that rode the entire length of the Yell-Mulberry county line, sheltering all that lay behind it from sight. Elliot, our dear protagonist of only thirty years of age, cured like leather by farmhand strength like his father, still had another fifteen minutes of drive time before he reached the tree line. Knowing he was coming to the end of a long two-day drive, Elliot sank back into the dirty, crushed velvet seat of his blue 1982 Buick Park Avenue, and with the coolest of archery, tossed a Lucky Strike between his lips and clinked open his silver zippo. The sharp orange flame licked the end of the cigarette, sending the smooth blue smoke down the cylindrical paper tube, waltzing briefly past his tongue as two couples twirl past each other on a ballroom floor, before being dutifully vacuumed down to the most eager chambers of his lungs.

It is in these long blocks of idle time, as in a waiting room, sitting in a bed engulfed by insomnia, or on long quiet drives across barren open country, that our minds begin to unwittingly drift; as a sailor that falls asleep at the helm, allowing the ship to drift in whatever direction the wind should take it. Along these still banks of Lethe, the mind glides effortlessly with no range nor bearing to heed, nor crew to oversee. No rudder being manned that would prevent you from some idle mishap as a result of your thought gazing. Just like the idle mishap that was about to yank Elliot from his torpid cruise.

Since the age of fifteen, Elliot has manned the wheel along this lonely stretch of highway. He had no other choice you see, as it was the only road that led anywhere beyond the boundaries of his little home town. He would toil up and down this road in his father's farm truck to pick up and deliver horse feed. He had taken this road to high school every day. He'd taken this very road at the age of seventeen to pick up his nonexistent prom date. Every bullet hole riddled speed limit sign, every pothole and deformity of the pavement, the flanks of the asphalt hugging mile after mile of neatly plowed dirt. It was as familiar to him as his own sun-beaten reflection in the mirror. Therefore, it should not surprise you, dear reader, idle witness to the events that are about to unfold, that Elliot would cock his head like a puzzled puppy upon seeing a well-established, two-storey brick office building in the near distance, that wasn't there two days ago.

"Oh what the fuck," he blurted, fearing he had somehow made a wrong turn. A small animal such as a rabbit, on its own home range, on its most familiar of runs would notice with ease the slightest of oddity. Be it the recent scent of a predator, the stink of a human, the unnatural loop of a poorly placed snare, or a fresh serving of bait. Should you come home one afternoon to find a freshly baked apple pie sitting neatly in the middle of a hallway, you'd take extra notice. It takes the skill of an experienced hunter to mask the deception. A two-story brick building constructed in as many days. Impossible. But before the unlikely event of having become lost was confirmed in his mind, a medicinal sigh of relief blew his fear of having made a wrong turn out of the window along with his cigarette smoke. For barely brimming over the farthest field's end in front of him, Elliot could see the emerald tops of the poplars. Almost home. He'd ask his roommate, Martin, about the building when he got home.

The next ten minutes of driving brought forth two events.

The first being the mile marker he'd been anticipating for the last forty-eight hours that meant he was ten minutes from home. As Odysseus must have felt having finally washed up on the banks of Ithaka, a restorative pulse began to course through Elliot's veins as he breached the poplar curtain. His pedal foot grew strong, his posture straightened, and his road-weary eyelids shed their weight. However, no sooner had he crossed that tree line threshold did the second event occur, buckling Elliot's new posture, pulling the plug from his stomach, discharging hope and draining the color from his skin.

The town of Yell. A cozy little serving of Americana with a meager population of 1,109 souls that could boast four churches, five bars, two genuine straight razor barbers and 'the longest running Dairy Queen in the state'. American flags waved like certificates of patriotic constituency at nearly every storefront. The long plastic road banners adorning Main Street with little 'u's cut through them so the harvest winds wouldn't blow them away; the colonial courthouse that centerpieced town square, the candy store, the ice cream parlor, the bookstore and antique shops that encompassed it. The water tower with the high school mascot painted on its side; Yell's odd souls and familiar routines, and all of the landmarks and warm idiosyncrasies that made it home are what Elliot expected to see but didn't. For hiding there behind the tall foliage of the county line, almost as if by some peculiar instance of macropsia, was not our cozy little town.

Four and five-storey buildings. Ten- and twenty-storey buildings. Wide sidewalks bustling with thousands of people, shopkeepers sweeping off their front walks, delivery trucks making their rounds, cafes, boutiques, hotels, theaters — all alive with faces and commerce. After roughly a solid thirty seconds of repetitively screaming, "Goddamn it," with each obscenity married to a corresponding punch to the steering wheel, and coming to terms with the fact that he'd been driving in the wrong direction for who knows how long, Elliot decided to pull in somewhere for coffee and directions.

Under the broad, immense towers that seem to have been constructed specifically to challenge the sky, with their summits scraping the passing clouds, and the permanent shadows they cast down like a curse, choking off all sunlight from the tireless rivers of life that coursed through the streets below, Elliot could feel himself inadvertently converting to the pulse of the city's congestion. The stopping and going of the cars and the heaving of their engines. The herds of pedestrians that flowed in synchro and the gallop of their breathing. With each rhythmic beat of the hearts and motors that pulsated within the guts of this titanic metropolis, the lanes seemed to narrow, and the cars seemed to ride a little closer. The very functions of Elliot's own lungs began to heed to the choking urban cadence. When all of a sudden, as with the first wave of a morphine drip, a familiar sidewalk sign up the street caught Elliot's eye and tugged on the reins of the overwhelming spectacle that surrounded him.

'Joe's Coffee', the sign read with an acquainted wink. Joe's Coffee was Elliot's favorite coffee shop back home in Yell, and noticing an empty parking space at its front, he wasted no time pulling in. Exhausted but resolved, he walked through the front door of the coffee house, taking in his surroundings with the apprehensiveness of a lost child. As peculiar as Elliot's situation was, the blue and white checkered tiles of the dining room walls, the little round bistro tables with matching tablecloths and the blue and white striped soda jerk paper hats the employees wore, to the Joe's Coffee company font on the daily specials board displaying the latest java-donut combos in fat comic book style letters of cadet blue; it all had a calming familiarity. And standing there at the self-serve pot, pouring himself a large to go, Elliot began to collect his thoughts.

'I must have not been paying attention.'
    Nine sugar packets.

'I need to call Martin.'

Five creamer packets.

'Cigarettes. I need cigarettes.'

One lid.

"What's the name of this place, buddy?"

"Joe's Coffee," the chubby kid with the dirty apron replied, as he punched the price for Elliot's coffee into the register.

"Oh sorry man, I meant the town. What's the name of this town?"

"Ah. Yell. This is Yell."

Elliot stared blankly for a moment, as if waiting for the punchline to a joke that he was in no mood for.

"No, seriously, what town is this?"

"Seriously, sir, this is Yell."

Elliot maintained his unapproving gaze. The chubby cashier returned a look of mocking parody.

"You're not about to ask me what year it is, are you?"

"Pardon me?" Elliot snapped.

"Nothing. Will that be all, sir? Just the coffee?" the kid responded, losing interest in the conversation.

"No. A pack of Luckies too."

Fuck it, Elliot thought to himself. I'll just ask someone who isn't a little prick.

"That payphone outside work?"

"Sure does, sir."

Elliot slapped the money on the counter, took his change and walked out. Standing at the curb next to the payphone in front of his car, swirling his coffee cup in a stirring motion and gazing at his urban surroundings with weary agitation, confusion and something very near to that thing called fear began to nestle in around him. Before his very eyes, the grey, shade shrouded streets began bowing to a deep purple with the drowning of late afternoon sun. The top windows of the tallest buildings began to reflect dusk's ribbons of fiery orange light, beaming them out like lighthouses far past his line of sight, towards a horizon Elliot was presently hidden from. The energetic colors of the neon signs, the flooding glow of street lamps and shop windows, the flashing Do Not Walk signs and the lights and blinkers of the cars, all began to bestow their living colors on the sidewalks and boulevards, projecting glowing watercolor-like paintings onto their concrete canvases. Elliot gripped the change in his pocket from the coffee so tightly that the freshly minted grooved edges of the dimes were beginning to cut into the tendons of his fingers.

"You all right, man?"

Startled, Elliot jumped and turned at the unexpected presence behind him. A tall homeless man with dark, shaggy hair stood humbly at a short distance behind him. His tattered clothes, his frail crooked hands, his sunken face, weathered, stained by street grime and loss. His eyes were dark and recessed but kind, tender-hearted and sad. And standing there hunched over by the weight of his life on his shoulders and the duffle bag on his back, he began to apologize.

"Sorry. I didn't mean to scare you. Are you all right?"

"What?" Elliot replied, gathering himself. "Yeah, I think so."

"You sure? You look like you're about to either puke

or shit your pants. Not so good maybe. You ought to sit down."

"Thanks, but I think I'm okay. What city am I in?"

"Puke it is then," he laughed. "I was right. I remember those days."

The homeless man paused for a moment, evaluating Elliot.

"Say, you got a light?" the transient continued, holding up a half-smoked cigarette.

"Sure. Here."

"Thanks." His frail knuckles whitened as he gripped Elliot's zippo, clinking it open and sparking its flint blackened wheel.

"Mmm. That's good," he muttered to himself as he brought the half-spent cigarette back to life. Snapping the lighter shut with a quick jerk of his wrist, he handed the lighter back to Elliot.

"So?" Elliot probed.

"So what?"

"So what city is this? Where the fuck am I at?"

"Oh. Say, you got any change man? Even just a few dimes."

"If you tell me what city this is."

"Yell. You're in Yell. The city of."

Elliot could only stare at the man with awkward confusion. He said Yell too. But before Elliot's natural, level-headed nature could prompt a challenge to the transient's answer, a yawning scream from behind him, like an air raid siren, swung Elliot's head around with the swift oscillation of a weathervane. As his eyes caught the bright red letters on the side of the van as it sped by, Elliot mouthed the words they read.

AMBULANCE
CITY OF YELL EMS

In stunned bewilderment, Elliot pulled the change he still had gripped in his fist and dropped the coins into the homeless man's already outstretched hand.

"Hey, thanks, man!" the transient shouted, as Elliot turned quickly away and made a hurried pace for his car.

Paranoia. Everyone will experience it at least once in the course of their lives. Me. You, my faithful reader. Everyone. On its surface, paranoia is a seemingly natural enough inevitability that once it is detected, our mind will automatically begin to prescribe a dismissal at anything that gives our fears a single tooth of strength in order to regain some sense of control over our mental faculties. It's a mind's attempt at curing this disorder of itself. But the only real cure for paranoia, is time. Time to allow the neurochemical processes to settle down. Time to breathe. Time to allow the left side of your brain to calm and console the right. Time to let the coffee do its work. Elliot slammed the door as he got back into his car in much the same manner that a child pulls the blankets over its head when frightened, started the engine, lit a trembling cigarette, drew a heavy sip of coffee and sat there. Staring at the homeless man as he trudged away, very real fear began to wrap itself around Elliot's bones like a frost. His hands and fingers trembled like guitar strings. "Fuck it," he blurted, trying to force himself to regain composure. "I got myself into this somehow. I can get myself out." Putting the cigarette in his mouth and the car into drive,

Elliot jutted back out onto the congested streets in an attempt to simply leave the city the same way he came in. It took him the better part of five minutes to get himself turned around. Traffic had now doubled. He could see the edge of the city where he had come in a way down the street. Ten blocks at most. But no car seemed to be able to move. Each shiny chrome bumper nearly biting the next. Headlights so close to the rear of the next car that their beams only lit the few inches of space between them. The only thing boasting movement was the homeless man a little way ahead, who had managed to find himself a run between the cars, allowing him to maze through and between the narrow iron ravines of shiny painted quarter panels and polished chrome, scraping his shins against the license plates as he passed, before vanishing like a breath on the wind into the crowded sidewalks. But not before a break in those crowds revealed not only the homeless man's escape, but Elliot's as well. A small alleyway a mere thirty feet up on the right, whose deep gaping silhouette was revealed only momentarily behind the bright reaching glares of the neon signs in the windows as the transient passed in front of them. A small solar eclipse of man and light revealing what was right in front of him. The alley was just big enough for a car, and if it connected to a parallel street with less traffic, perhaps he could get moving again. Putting the car in reverse and cutting the wheel, Elliot tried to notch his Buick at just enough of an angle that he could pull up onto the sidewalk.

"I don't know you, and I don't owe you. You fuckers are just going to have to move," he barked at the unsuspecting commuters as he heaped the front tire up onto the curb. The large beast of American automotive workmanship lugged up onto the sidewalk, parting the small river of shoppers and pedestrians as a shark parts a school of fish, and weaved its way up to the edge of the alleyway.

No sooner was Elliot committed upon turning down into the alley, now flanked tightly on either side by the towering concrete walls of the buildings, did he realize he could not see another avenue on the other side. The forging beams of his headlights only evaporated into the darkness of the alley ahead. And no sooner still, did the car that was behind him in traffic decide to follow suit, tucking in behind him as if the driver felt that Elliot knew some sort of detour or short cut around the clogged streets. "I really hope you're not counting on me to get you out of this, pal." Pushing deeper into the alley in the hopes there would be some place to turn around, Elliot drove on. With the walls becoming narrower the deeper he braved into the alley, and the car following behind him so closely, only a frosting of light around the edges of Elliot's rear window would let one know there was a car behind him. "You really need to get off my—" Elliot slammed on his brakes so hard the pedal nearly seized. Dead end. No more alleyway. No place to turn around. "FUCK!" Elliot screamed the obscenity with such vocal force that the blood rushed to his head, momentarily blurring his vision.

The idea of torture is terrifying. We often think of it as a mode of interrogation, or as a means of punishment. Helplessness. Trapped. Hands and feet bound. Fingers being broken. Skin being flayed. The exploitation of phobias. Sleep deprivation. Teeth being pulled. Sawing and scalping. No escape. But there is another form of torture. One that we often self-administer more willingly than that which we would have applied to ourselves as a criminal or prisoner of war. A manner of self-torture that we frequently drown ourselves in, often in the midst of repetitive failure, the perpetual absence of accomplishment in any given matter. Again, we find ourselves trapped. Hands and feet bound by ropes of our own shortcomings. Our mental and emotional appendages that we use to feel around for an escape or solution being cauterized or dismembered by our previous failures. Yet we continue to struggle, to free ourselves like a trapped rabbit from a snare. To find a way to cut the ropes that bind us and finally escape. Elliot threw up his hands in a loss, motioning to the driver behind him that there was nowhere else to go. Seeing no headlights rearing away, Elliot reached up and clicked on his overhead light so the driver could see him better, then repeated his flailings in another effort to get the driver to back up. Still, the tailgater made no retreat. Elliot couldn't even make out the glow from the driver's headlights any more. "Fine," Elliot said as he wrenched open the door handle. He was only able to jar the door open about a foot before it chipped against the solid brick of the alley wall. Begrudgingly, Elliot wedged himself out of the door jam and turned his head toward the rear of the car. But before any motorist to motorist chastising could escape his lips, the weight of disbelief dropped down like an anvil and buckled his knees, forcing Elliot to catch himself against the pinned door. There was no other car behind him. There was only a wall. Elliot stood frozen. The very air in his lungs; the thump of his heart; the taillights of Elliot's car and the candy red light they cast, all held firmly in the petrified bosom of shock induced suspended animation.

A recent publication by Harvard Medical School describes the human fight or flight response as, *a stressful incident that can make the heart pound and breathing quicken. Muscles tense and beads of sweat appear. The fight or flight response evolved as a survival mechanism, enabling humans and other mammals to react quickly to life threatening situations. The carefully orchestrated, yet near instantaneous sequence of hormonal changes and physiological responses help someone to either fight off a threat or flee to safety. Unfortunately, the body can also overreact to stressors that are not life threatening.* It is in this definition, that we shall reanimate our dear Elliot.

A grate. Breaking free of his macabre paralyses, Elliot noticed a tall slender grate, no wider or taller than himself with heavy wrought iron bars, as those used in the straining of trash and debris from municipal waterways, neatly nestled in the corner wall in front of his car. With fight or flight taking hold, Elliot climbed onto the top of his car, the hood buckling and plunking as he made his way to the front end. Reeling his foot back, and with the full weight of his body, Elliot thrust his foot forward like a battering ram toward the grate, driving kick after solid kick at the iron bars, shuddering its hinges in the mortar.

With each lunging kick, the grate rattled more and

more before finally snapping off its two heavy hinges and falling back into the darkness with an echoing crash. Pausing only to allow his eyes to adjust to the darkness of the tunnel that the now defeated grate had guarded, he stepped carefully down off the hood and into the blackness of the narrow pathway. No sooner had his eyes adjusted, Elliot noticed a soft glow of light reflecting off the stone of the walls ahead, revealing a turn a mere ten feet in front of him. With the same boost of restorative energy we get when we see the finish line at the end of a long race, when after a long day's work we look at the clock to discover we only have ten more minutes left on our shift, or, seeing an exit sign or familiar roadside feature at the end of a long drive, letting you know you're almost home, Elliot's pulse began to course and thump. His legs grew stronger. His posture straightened. A sugar spoon of hope. With a boost of fortitude and pupils the size of pennies, he made his way around the corner, into the slightly narrower corridor that it led to, step by cautious step. A similar glow, reflecting off the walls at the end of this second passage revealed another turn, with an identical glow at its ending. Fearing this would only continue, Elliot lost his nerve and turned to go back the way he had come, and would have done so, had the corridor not closed in behind him. Once again, there would be no going back the way he had come.

There is another step, ladies and gentlemen. Another branch extending out from the fight or flight response to sudden life or death traumas. For what if death were in fact certain? Or in the least perceived to be. We will assume that most people would succumb to one of the two following outcomes. One, which would surmise to a sort of primal, fight anyway and die standing in the throes of ancient combat type reaction. To smash the chains of the fear of death. One final injection of adrenaline to finish the job. The second outcome would be an either despairing, or peaceful, passive acceptance of mortality, losing all ego, lowering your head and dropping to your knees at peace with inevitability. Elliot succumbed to the despairing version of that second outcome. Upon trying to escape and finding nothing but another wall, he knew what had happened. You do as well. The walls had been closing in behind him, like patient assassins closing in on their target, step by insidious step. Elliot was entombed.

It is a terrible thing to hear a grown man scream. All airs of any masculinity are stripped away, leaving a bare defenseless soul, floundering in a puddle of helplessness. A strong proven ship's captain with a gut full of seawater is reduced to nothing more than a weak, defenseless goldfish on the stage of fear. A sincere full-throated scream, born in the guts of dread and alarm in an enclosed space cuts the eardrum like a scalpel and persists long after the sound has been produced. Darkness, confusion, irresolution and terror ripped through Elliot's very mortal being like a tank round and then ejected its spent shell, hope, his very soul to the ground with a heavy, hollow thud. And now Elliot's own desperate screams were attacking him with virulence.

"Hello?"

"I heard someone."

"HEY!"

There is always a silver lining. The laws of probability indicate that within the rules of cause and effect, even the worst, most catastrophic of events will have a good or positive event that will rise somewhere as a direct result. The way a death can bring a family closer together. How not getting one job allowed you to accidentally get a better one. The way that getting a speeding ticket made you late and prevented you from boarding that fateful flight. Or in this case, the way the inability to scream loud enough, allows another sound to be heard.

A voice. It's muffled. Too muffled to make out words.

"HEY!" Elliot screamed, slapping his hands against the wall and hoping he would at least produce a similar muffled sound on the other side. "HELLO!" Elliot repeated. "HELP ME! I'M IN HERE!"

The muffled voice was becoming slightly more pronounced. Sounds like it is saying, "All be it."

"I'M IN HERE! Elliot screamed.

"All be it."

"All be it."

"HEY! HELLO!" Elliot frantically began squirming with anticipation while continuing to scream, slap and claw his hands against the black wall. Breathing heavily from his jolt of hope, he began gulping the last few trace amounts of oxygen in his tomb, and a dizziness crept over him ever so gently. Though he could see nothing he could feel his eyes growing heavy. His arms and legs began to tingle, then fall asleep, and a peaceful loss of consciousness wrapped around him like a mellow spring wind, leaving him floating in a physical quiescence, like a ribbon of smoke in a still room.

"All be it."

"All be it."

"Blood king, is it.

"BLOOD KING IS IT!"

"FUCKING IDIOT!" The voice cleared, a sudden rush of light filled Elliot's eyes and a pinching, vice-like pain gripped his arm with the ferociousness of a dog bite. A mattress was brushing across his face, and whatever had him by the arm was now dragging him across the floor. "Elliot! You fucking idiot! What the hell are you doing?" his roommate, Martin, shouted, dragging Elliot out from underneath his bed. Elliot just laid there on the floor, panting like a dog. His shirt covered in sweat. The needle still in his arm. His roommate stared down at him in complete despisement. After a short moment, the huffing and puffing began to subside and a slight, mischievous grin began to draw across Elliot's pale face. "Don't fucking smile at me, asshole. It's disgusting. You've got problems, man. You've no reason to smile," his roommate barked as he stormed out of Elliot's room, slamming the door behind him. Elliot jumped to his feet, pulled the needle from his arm, walked over to his old wooden desk where his typewriter sat and lit a cigarette. Writer's block cured. Elliot started typing.

Madd Man
by Elliot Madd

Across these limitless, umber brown fields of rich farm soil that stretch out in every direction, to distances only comparable to the sapphire skies that envelope them, time and space seem to intertwine so effortlessly that they become one, unstoppable, force.

THE END